MW01114483

RAY KROC

Gloria D. Miklowitz

Đ Dominie Press, Inc.

Publisher: Raymond Yuen
Editor: John S. F. Graham
Designer: Greg DiGenti
Photo Credits: Bettmann/Corbis (pages 6, 15, 21, 28, and cover)

Published by:

⌐ᗡ Dominie Press, Inc.

1949 Kellogg Avenue
Carlsbad, California 92008 USA

www.dominie.com

Paperback ISBN 0-7685-1220-4
Library Bound Edition ISBN 0-7685-1545-9
Printed in Singapore by PH Productions Pte Ltd
  2 3 4 5 6 PH 04 03

Table of Contents

Chapter 1

A Smile and Enthusiasm

Have you ever eaten at McDonald's? How about a hamburger and fries and maybe a big chocolate milkshake?

The name "McDonald's" is known throughout the world. Since 1957, when Ray Kroc opened his first McDonald's, the worldwide chain of restaurants has sold billions of hamburgers.

Ray Kroc, founder of the McDonald's Corporation

How did it all begin?

Ray Kroc was born in Chicago in 1902. His father, Louis Kroc, had to leave school when he was twelve to help support his widowed mother and family. For most of his life, he worked for the American District Telegraph Company. Ray's mother, Rose, taught piano, and Ray was one of her best students.

"I was never much of a reader when I was a boy," Ray said. "I liked action." His mother called him "Danny Dreamer" because he spent a lot of time thinking, often about ways to make money. One of his first ventures was to sell lemonade. While still in elementary school, he worked at a grocery store and then at his uncle's drugstore. There he learned, "you could influence people with a smile and enthusiasm and sell them a sundae when they'd come for a cup of coffee."

Ray got as much pleasure out of work as he did from playing baseball. School bored him, but he did enjoy debating, which he was very good at. Though only fifteen, he dropped out of high school, believing he could make his way in the world without graduating. It was 1917, and the United States had entered World War I. Ray signed up as a Red Cross ambulance driver.

The war ended before Ray went overseas. Still a teenager, he chose to do what he liked and could do best— selling things and playing the piano. His first job was selling novelties. At night he played piano for extra money. In a short time he was earning more than his father. The job he liked most was playing the piano at a summer resort on Paw-Paw Lake, Michigan. "We were really with it," he said, "in our striped blazers and straw boater hats."

There, at seventeen, he met and fell in love with Ethel Fleming, whose parents owned a hotel across the lake. A year later, he told his father he wanted to marry her. "Not until you hold a steady job," he was told. A few days later, Ray went to work for the Lily Tulip Company, selling something new to America—paper cups. Now that he was earning a living, he and Ethel could be married.

Chapter 2

Paper Cups and Milkshake Makers

As a married man, Ray was determined to earn a good living. From early morning until five or five-thirty at night, he sold paper cups to soda fountains and restaurants. He played piano at a radio station from six to eight at night, and then again from

ten to two in the morning. With only
a few hours of sleep, he was up again,
selling cups.

He was a good salesman, but cup
sales slowed in Chicago's winter. Then
he learned that there was plenty of
work in Florida selling empty lots for
homes. He said, "Only an alligator
could love" some of the land for sale.
But Ray decided to take a break from
his job selling cups. He drove to Miami
with his wife Ethel, their baby girl, and
Ethel's sister.

Miami was packed with people
trying to make money. Ray quickly
found work with a real estate firm and
persuaded many Chicago visitors to buy
land—until the real estate boom ended.

He found work playing piano in a

fancy Miami nightclub called The Silent Night. The club eventually closed. Ethel, alone each night with their daughter, missed her family in Chicago. Ray decided to go home, back to his old job.

In 1926, Ray returned to the Lily Tulip Company. He was always thinking up new ways to sell cups. For example, he persuaded the Walgreen drugstore chain to offer take-out food at its lunch counters. They would need paper cups for drinks that customers took with them. Not only were more lunches sold during rush hour, but Ray doubled his sales of paper cups.

At Ray's urging, the Prince Castle chain of ice cream parlors improved their milkshake recipe. People loved the new taste and bought more shakes.

Soon Ray was selling a million Lily cups a year to the chain.

When Ray's father died in 1932, Ray found a yellowed paper, dated 1906, among his father's things. It was a report from a phrenologist, a person who tells your future from the bumps on your head. The report predicted that four-year-old Raymond A. Kroc would work in some kind of food service. The prediction was already coming true.

Chapter 3

The McDonald Brothers

The owner of Prince Castle ice cream parlors was a mechanical engineer. He designed a mixing machine that could make five milkshakes at once. It was called the Multimixer. Ray was very impressed. The more Multimixers in use, the more milkshakes would be made

Ray Kroc at his desk at company headquarters in Chicago, Illinois

and the more paper cups he would be able to sell. He wanted Lily Tulip to sign up to distribute the Multimixer, but Lily said no.

Convinced the Multimixer would make money, Ray took a big risk. He refinanced his home and borrowed nearly $100,000 to buy the mixer distributing rights. Frightened by the risk, Ethel refused to help, even in the office.

Ray's new company, started in 1941, did very well until the United States entered World War II. Then, copper needed for the mixer motors was required for the war effort. And sugar, for ice cream, was in short supply. Always resourceful, Ray found substitutes that imitated the taste and texture of ice cream.

The Multimixer business did very well again until after the war ended and lifestyles changed. Soldiers returning from the war got married, bought homes, and moved to suburbs, miles from drugstore soda fountains. Young families now drove to inexpensive restaurants to eat.

About this time, Ray noticed something odd. Most fast-food outlets ordered only one or two Multimixers, except in San Bernardino, California. There, two brothers named Dick and Maurice "Mac" McDonald bought eight Multimixers for their hamburger stand. Eight Multimixers could make forty shakes at a time! What were they doing that required so many machines?

Ray decided to go to San Bernardino to find out.

Chapter 4

What's the Attraction Here?

Ray drove from Chicago to San Bernardino. At about ten in the morning, he cruised past the McDonalds' eight-sided building. It was an ordinary looking drive-in restaurant. He was not impressed.

An hour later, workers began appearing—men dressed in what Ray called "spiffy white shirts and trousers, with white paper hats." They started moving supplies from a storage shed into the building—cartons of meat, sacks of potatoes, cases of milk and soft drinks, and boxes of buns. Soon they were bustling around "like ants at a picnic."

Before noon, people began arriving to stand in line. "What's the attraction here?" Ray asked a man waiting to order his lunch.

"You'll get the best hamburger you ever ate for fifteen cents," the man said. "And you don't have to wait and mess around tipping waitresses."

It was a hot day, but no flies swarmed around the place. The workers kept everything neat and clean as they worked. Even the parking lot was free of litter.

Ray returned later to speak with the owners, Dick and Mac McDonald, who knew him as "Mr. Multimixer." They explained that they only sold hamburgers and cheeseburgers. Burgers were a tenth of a pound of meat, all fried the same way, for fifteen cents. Cheese on the burger cost an additional four cents. Three ounces of fries and soft drinks were ten cents each. Sixteen-ounce milkshakes cost twenty cents, and a cup of coffee cost one nickel.

They showed Ray plans they'd had drawn for a new building with a golden arch through the roof and big windows. It would have bathrooms and a much-improved serving area. That night Ray

*Ray Kroc holds up a hamburger and a drink
in front of a McDonald's restaurant*

had visions of McDonald's restaurants all over the country, each with eight Multimixers whirring away—machines he would be able to sell with no trouble to them.

The next day, Ray returned to watch how the French fries were prepared, how the griddle man handled his job—flattening each burger and scraping the sizzling griddle. After the lunch hour rush, Ray approached the McDonald brothers. "Why don't you open a series of drive-ins like this?" he asked. "It would be a gold mine for you and me." He imagined a hundred such restaurants. He could sell the McDonald brothers 800 Multimixers!

The brothers weren't interested. They had a nice home. In the evening they'd sit on their porch and watch the sunset.

They said, "We don't need any more problems than we have in keeping this place going."

"What if someone else operated the other places for you?" Ray asked.

"Who?" Dick wanted to know.

"How about me?" said Ray.

Chapter 5

Persistence and Determination

When the brothers agreed, Ray was very excited.

The first "model" McDonald's opened in Des Plaines, Illinois in March 1955, near Ray's home. He checked the restaurant each morning before going to his Multimixer office in downtown Chicago. On the way home he stopped again, picking up every McDonald's wrapper and cup on the ground. Though he was president of his Multimixer company, on weekends he hosed down the new drive-in parking lot, scrubbed trashcans, and scraped chewing gum off the concrete.

In the next year, eleven new McDonald's opened. The most successful of those was in Waukegan, Illinois. The day after the doors opened, the manager ran out of cash register space for all the dollar bills that flooded in. Ten years later, almost 700 restaurants were operating, and the number was growing by 100 a year.

One innovation Ray began was Hamburger University. New McDonald's owners went there to learn how to cook fries and hamburgers to exact specifications. He compared his "university" to Harvard and Stanford, and students could get degrees in *hamburgerology*.

With the help of Harry J. Sonneborn, a financial wizard, Ray bought out the McDonald brothers' contract for almost $3 million dollars! Then, to raise more money to expand, he decided to sell shares in his company. McDonald's sold shares on the stock market at $22.50 each. In one day, they rose to $30 and soared to almost $50. One hundred shares bought in 1965 for $2,250 would be worth $2.5 million at the end of 2000.

Over the next several years, McDonald's became as well-known as Coca-Cola. Thousands of new restaurants opened in the United States and other countries. Ray Kroc became a very rich man. However, his long work hours and other problems led to a divorce from Ethel, and later his second wife.

Joan Smith became his third wife and great love. They were married in Hawaii on March 8, 1969.

In 1974, Ray bought a baseball team, the San Diego Padres. He lectured at Dartmouth College, where he was given an honorary doctorate. He celebrated his 70th birthday by giving $7 million to Chicago's Lincoln Park Zoo, Children's Memorial Hospital, and the church he attended as a child, Harvard Congregational Church in Oak Park, Illinois. He established the Kroc

*The San Diego Chicken with Ray Kroc and
his wife, Joan, at a baseball game*

Foundation to research diabetes and
arthritis (both of which he had) and
multiple sclerosis, which his sister
Loraine had. He has received dozens of
awards for his amazing achievements.

Asked what he attributed his success
to, Ray said, "Determination. Nothing
in the world can take the place of

persistence. Talent will not—nothing is more common than unsuccessful men with talent. Genius will not—unrewarded genius is almost a proverb. Education will not—the world is full of educated derelicts. Persistence and determination alone are omnipotent."

Ray Kroc died of a heart disorder in 1979. Today, there are over 28,000 McDonald's restaurants in 120 countries serving 45 million people a day.

Glossary

Ambulance - an emergency vehicle that transports people who are injured or very sick to a hospital.

Arthritis - a disease of the bones that makes movement very painful.

Attorney - lawyer.

Attributed - the reason why; given credit for.

Blazer - a suit jacket.

Bustling - having a lot of activity.

Dartmouth - a small college in New Hampshire, one of the "Ivy League" schools.

Derelict - an unemployed person who does not want to work (slang)

Determination - moving forward with force.

Diabetes - a disease of the pancreas where sugar that you eat can't be used by the body. Usually, sugar is used as energy by the body, but if it isn't used, it builds up in the bloodstream. If there is too much sugar in the bloodstream, a person can get very sick.

Established - started.

Financial - having to do with money.

Griddle - a type of large frying pan.

Honorary Doctorate - a degree given by universities and colleges to someone who has accomplished something great, even though they haven't attended or finished the required schoolwork.

Influence - to change by doing or saying something to someone.

Multiple Sclerosis - a disease of the brain that causes malfunctions of many different systems in the body, including the eyes, the muscles, the skin, and memory.

Novelties - small, usually attractive, things that have a limited use.

Omnipotent - the most powerful.

Persistence - to keep on going.

Phrenologist - someone who claims to tell the future by "reading" bumps on the head. In the 1890s and 1900s, people thought that the shape of a person's head determined their fate.

Proverb - a saying that presents a moral or a life lesson.

Refinance - to pay off a loan by taking out another loan.

Resourceful - having the ability to find solutions to problems.

Rights - permission. When someone "buys the rights" to something, they are getting permission to use it in a way that helps them make money.

Shares - parts of a company. A company can sell shares on the stock market to raise money. This means that people can own a part of the company if they buy shares of it. Over the years, the price of the shares goes up and down according to what people think the company is worth.

Soda fountains - types of restaurants that serve soda, ice cream, and milkshakes at a counter.

Spiffy - well-dressed, neat, and clean (slang).

Straw Boater Hats - a round hat made of straw that was popular with musicians in the 1930s and 1940s.

Trousers - pants.

Ventures - businesses that may be risky.

Widowed - when a spouse dies. A woman is widowed when her husband dies.